STORYWORLDS

Richard Brown

Oliver & Boyd

Acknowledgements
We are grateful to the following for giving permission to reproduce extracts from copyright works: A. & C. Black Ltd, for 'The Twelve Days of Christmas' by students of Mausica College, Trinidad, from *Mango Spice* (ed. by Conolly, Cameron, Singham); Basil Blackwell Ltd, from *Annie, the Invisible Girl*, by Ruth Thomson; The Bodley Head, for 'Happy Birthday, Dilroy' and 'If I Could Only Take Home a Snowflake' from *I Din Do Nuttin* by John Agard; Victor Gollancz Ltd, for 'The Pudding Like a Night on the Sea' from *The Julian Stories* by Ann Cameron illustrations © Ann Strugnell 1981; Hamish Hamilton Ltd, from *The Cherry Tree* by Ruskin Bond illustrations by Valerie Littlewood; Harrap Ltd, for 'The Mouse Girl' and 'Lo Sun, the Blind Boy' adapted by Richard Brown, from *Folk Tales of All Nations* (ed. by F. Lee); William Heinemann Ltd, for 'The Woman, the Boy and the Lion' from *The Story Spirits* by A Williams-Ellis; Julia MacRae Books, from *Linda's Lie* by Bernard Ashley; Methuen's Children's Books, from *Chin Chiang and the Dragon Dance* by Ian Wallace; Grace Nicholls, from *Trust You Wriggly*; Young World Books for 'Our City', 'Some People', 'My Friends', 'My Grandfather in Cyprus' and 'My Island Dream' from *Our City* (ed. by L. Searle).

Every effort has been made to contact copyright holders, but in some cases it has been impossible to do so. We apologise for any infringement that may have inadvertently occurred.

We are also grateful to the following for supplying photographs and giving permission for their use: The Anthony Blake Photo Library (p 29); The J. Allan Cash Photolibrary (pp 32–33, 41, 68–69, 80–81); Stephanie Colasanti (p 40).

Illustrated by Jaquie Thomas, Bob Geary, Janet McKay, Tamasin Cole, Gwen Tourret, Peter Dennis, Joanna Troughton, Joanna Williams, and Andrew Brownfoot

Oliver & Boyd
Robert Stevenson House
1–3 Baxter's Place
Leith Walk
Edinburgh EH1 3BB

A Division of Longman Group UK Ltd

© Oliver & Boyd 1988. The acknowledgements above constitute an extension of this copyright line.

First published 1988
ISBN 0 05 004200 9
Set in Linotron Plantin 14 on 18pt and Linotron Univers 12 on 16pt
Produced by Longman Group (FE) Ltd
Printed in Hong Kong

Contents

Annie,
the Invisible Girl

Once upon a time there was a little girl called
Annie.   She lived in a tiny house in a quiet
valley.

There was a hill on either side of the valley.
At the top of one hill was a village called
Greenville.

Annie lived in the middle.   At the top of the
other hill was a village called Blueville.

The children of Greenville were mean.
Instead of playing games they were cruel to
animals.   They hated the children of Blueville.

The children of Blueville were just as unfair. They spoiled flowers and cut down trees. They hated the children of Greenville.

The children of Greenville were always fighting the children of Blueville. The children of Blueville were always fighting the children of Greenville.

Annie always stayed safely inside her house whenever there was fighting. "I wish they wouldn't fight," she thought, "because I would like to play with them."

She had to play by herself. She was happy playing with the animals and the plants. But she really wanted to be friends with the other children.

The children of Greenville were cruel to her because she wasn't green. They set traps for her and laughed when she fell in.

And the children of Blueville were cruel to her because she wasn't blue. They chased after her and called her nasty names.

Annie tried to be friendly with all the children but none of them wanted to be friends. She took presents to Greenville. They took no notice of her because she wasn't green.

She went to Blueville dressed in blue clothes, but it made no difference.

Annie felt very, very lonely. She sat down by the river and cried. She cried so much that a strange thing happened. She began to disappear.

That night, the Greenville children set a trap for the Blueville children. They thought nobody could see them; but they didn't know about Annie.

She put up warning signs. In the morning, the Greenville children were amazed. The Blueville children didn't mind. And Annie smiled.

The Blueville children made a secret weapon for throwing stones at the Greenville children. They thought nobody could see them; but they didn't know about Annie.

She untied the string and threw the weapon

away.   The Blueville children couldn't understand what had happened.   The Greenville children didn't mind.   And Annie smiled.

Each time the Greenville children thought of another nasty trick, Annie upset their plans.

In the end, the Greenville children found better things to do.   They found that animals were nice after all.   And Annie's smile got bigger.

Now that the fighting had stopped, the Blueville children also found better things to do.   They started growing things and looking after them.

One day some Greenville children met some Blueville children. For the first time they saw each other smiling. They thought that being friends would be fun.

The children all came to play near Annie's house. When she saw that they were friends, Annie smiled more than ever. She smiled so much that a strange thing happened. She became visible again. Everyone let her join in their games.

Now Annie likes living in between Greenville and Blueville.

By Ruth Thomson

Hamid and the Weight-Lifter

In Persia, long ago, there was a busy market
place.   Not only did they sell all their best
wares there – fine cloths and oil and pots – but
many Persians came to the market to perform:
acrobats, artists, singers, sculptors, tailors, and
so on.

One day a wise old man arrived in this
market place.   With him was his ten-year-old
grandson, Hamid.   The old man was tired and
thirsty, so he settled down on a box while his
grandson fetched him a drink.

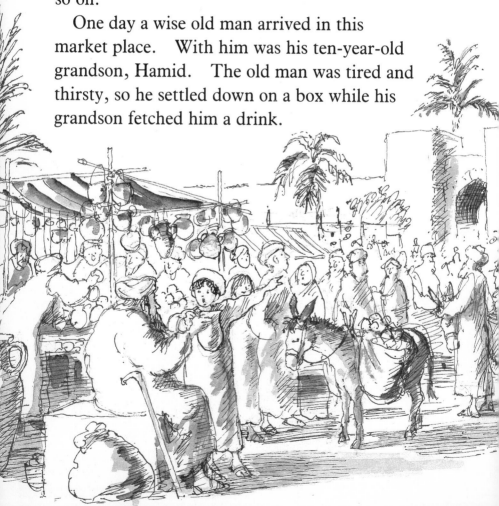

When Hamid returned with the water he looked excited. "There's a huge weight-lifter over there," he said. "I've never seen anyone lift so much. He must be stronger than an ox. Can we go and watch?"

They found a place in a large circle of people who had gathered to watch the weight-lifter. He was an enormous man, clad only in a loin-cloth, sandals, and a turban; and a great brown beard flowed almost to his navel.

He was making ready to lift a weight, which, he declared, was so heavy no man had ever lifted it. Someone in the audience scoffed at that. The weight-lifter glared; he stalked round the circle, seeking the scoffer, and no one dared move for fear of being singled out. The giant grinned; he invited three men to try together to lift the weight. Heave as they might, they could raise it only a few centimetres crookedly off the ground.

The whole market place grew hushed as the weight-lifter crouched, grasped the weight, and tensed his huge muscles.

The old man turned to whisper something to Hamid, but his grandson was no longer by his side. "Hamid?" he called as loud as he dared, looking around; several of the crowd shushed him; he had no choice but to turn back and watch.

The weight-lifter, visibly staggering, with sweat pouring down his face, heaved the weight onto his chest and then, with immense effort, above his head and held it there, grinning triumphantly. There was loud but respectful applause.

Dropping the weight, he trumpeted, "I'm the most powerful man in Persia." He waved his hands triumphantly above his head.

After the applause there was a silence. And in that silence came a mischievous and boyish voice, cutting through the air like bird song.

"The ox can pull a cart, and the elephant lift a man, but what *else* can they do?"

A ripple of surprise went through the circle,

and eyes searched for the hidden speaker. The weight-lifter glared furiously, tensing his body and closing his hands into fists.

The voice came again, "The ox is a slave, the elephant is dumb; and so are you."

The crowd whispered, smiled, chuckled, laughed, until there was an uproar of mirth. The weight-lifter, blood rushing to his face, stalked around the circle, bellowing furiously, "Who dares to say that to me? Let the scoundrel show himself."

The people edged away, still chuckling. Only the old man stayed where he was, alone, unafraid. The weight-lifter confronted him. "Was it you?" he threatened.

The old man shook his head.

"Then why are you smiling?"

"You say you are the most powerful man in the world," the wise old man replied. "And yet you can't bear the weight of a few unpleasant words."

The old man stared straight into the eyes of the weight-lifter, and slowly, the giant lowered his gaze. He turned away, knowing what a fool he had looked. No more would the Persians fear his strength and his wrath.

The old man hobbled off. Hamid suddenly appeared at his side. "Where were you?" his grandfather asked.

"Behind those bales of cloth.   But I saw everything."   And he winked at his grandfather.

The old man patted the head of his smiling grandson.   "You're a boy after my own heart," he said – and then he stopped still and laughed, his frail old body shaking.   Hamid stared at him in amusement, and then joined in; and you could hardly tell the difference between the two mischievous sounds.

A Persian Folk Tale
rewritten by RICHARD BROWN

Happy Birthday, Dilroy!

My name is Dilroy.
I'm a little black boy
and I'm eight today.

My birthday cards say
it's great to be eight
and they sure right
coz I got a pair of skates
I want for a long long time.

My birthday cards say,
Happy Birthday, Dilroy!
But, Mummy, tell me why
they don't put a little boy
that looks a bit like me.
Why the boy on the card so white?

JOHN AGARD

If I Could Only Take Home a Snowflake

Snowflakes
like tiny
insects drifting
down.

Without a hum
they come,
Without a hum
they go.

Snowflakes
like tiny
insects
drifting
down.

If only
I could take
one
home with me
to show
my friends
in the sun,
just for fun,
just for fun.

JOHN AGARD

The Pudding Like a Night on the Sea

"I'm going to make something special for your mother," my father said.

My mother was out shopping. My father was in the kitchen looking at the pots and the pans and the jars of this and that.

"What are you going to make?" I said.

"A pudding," he said.

My father is a big man with wild black hair. When he laughs, the sun laughs in the window-panes. When he thinks, you can almost see his thoughts sitting on all the tables and chairs. When he is angry, me and my little brother Huey shiver to the bottom of our shoes.

"What kind of pudding will you make?" Huey said.

"A wonderful pudding," my father said. "It will taste like a whole raft of lemons. It will taste like a night on the sea."

Then he took down a knife and sliced five lemons in half. He squeezed the first one. Juice squirted in my eye.

"Stand back!" he said, and squeezed again.

The seeds flew out on the floor. "Pick up those seeds, Huey!" he said.

Huey took the broom and swept them up.

My father cracked some eggs and put the yolks in a pan and the whites in a bowl. He rolled up his sleeves and pushed back his hair and beat up the yolks. "Sugar, Julian!" he said, and I poured in the sugar.

He went on beating. Then he put in lemon juice and cream and set the pan on the stove. The pudding bubbled and he stirred it fast. Cream splashed on the stove.

"Wipe that up, Huey!" he said.

Huey did.

It was hot by the stove. My father loosened his collar and pushed at his sleeves. The stuff in the pan was getting thicker and thicker. He held the beater up high in the air. "Just right!" he said, and sniffed in the smell of the pudding.

He whipped the egg whites and mixed them into the pudding. The pudding looked softer and lighter than air.

"Done!" he said. He washed all the pots, splashing water on the floor, and wiped the counter so fast his hair made circles around his head.

"Perfect!" he said. "Now I'm going to take a nap. If something important happens, bother me. If nothing important happens, don't bother me. And – the pudding is for your mother. Leave the pudding alone!"

He went to the living room and was asleep in

a minute, sitting straight up in his chair.

Huey and I guarded the pudding.

"Oh, it's a wonderful pudding," Huey said.

"With waves on the top like the ocean," I said.

"I wonder how it tastes," Huey said.

"Leave the pudding alone," I said.

"If I just put my finger in – there – I'll know how it tastes," Huey said.

And he did it.

"You did it!" I said.   "How does it taste?"

"It tastes like a whole raft of lemons," he said.

"It tastes like a night on the sea."

"You've made a hole in the pudding!" I said. "But since you did it, I'll have a taste."   And it tasted like a whole night of lemons.   It tasted like floating at sea.

"It's such a big pudding," Huey said. "It can't hurt to have a little more."

"Since you took more, I'll have more," I said.

"That was a bigger lick than I took!" Huey said. "I'm going to have more again."

"Whoops!" I said.

"You put in your whole hand!" Huey said. "Look at the pudding you spilled on the floor!"

"I am going to clean it up," I said. And I took the rag from the sink.

"That's not really clean," Huey said.

"It's the best I can do," I said.

"Look at the pudding!" Huey said.

It looked like craters on the moon. "We have to smooth this over," I said. "So it looks the way it did before! Let's get spoons."

And we evened the top of the pudding with spoons, and while we evened it, we ate some more.

"There isn't much left," I said.

"We were supposed to leave the pudding alone," Huey said.

"We'd better get away from here," I said. We ran into our bedroom and crawled under the bed. After a long time we heard my father's voice.

"Come into the kitchen, dear," he said. "I have something for you."

"Why, what is it?" my mother said, out in the kitchen.

Under the bed, Huey and I pressed ourselves to the wall.

"Look," said my father, out in the kitchen. "A wonderful pudding."

"Where is the pudding?" my mother said.

"WHERE ARE YOU BOYS?" my father said. His voice went through every crack and corner of the house.

We felt like two leaves in a storm.

"WHERE ARE YOU, I SAID!"

My father's voice was booming.

Huey whispered to me, "I'm scared."

We heard my father walking slowly through the rooms.

"Huey!" he called. "Julian!"

We could see his feet. He was coming into our room.

He lifted the bedspread. There was his face, and his eyes like black lightning. He grabbed us by the legs and pulled. "STAND UP!" he said.

We stood.

"What do you have to tell me?" he said.

"We went outside," Huey said, "and when we came back, the pudding was gone!"

"Then why were you hiding under the bed?" my father said.

We didn't say anything.   We looked at the
floor.

"I can tell you one thing," he said.   "There
is going to be some beating here now!   There is
going to be some whipping!"

The curtains at the window were shaking.
Huey was holding my hand.

"Go into the kitchen!" my father said.
"Right now!"

We went into the kitchen.

"Come here, Huey!" my father said.

Huey walked towards him, his hands behind
his back.

"See these eggs?" my father said. He cracked
them and put the yolks in a pan and set the pan
on the counter.   He stood a chair by the
counter.   "Stand up here," he said to Huey.

Huey stood on the chair by the counter.

"Now it's time for your beating!" my father
said.

Huey started to cry.   His tears fell in with
the egg yolks.

"Take this!" my father said.   My father
handed him the egg beater.   "Now beat those
eggs," he said.   "I want this to be a good
beating!"

"Oh!" Huey said.   He stopped crying.
And he beat the egg yolks.

"Now you, Julian, stand here!" my father said.

25

I stood on a chair by the table.

"I hope you're ready for your whipping!"

I didn't answer. I was afraid to say yes or no.

"Here!" he said, and he set the egg whites in front of me. "I want these whipped and whipped well!"

"Yes, sir!" I said, and started whipping.

My father watched us. My mother came into the kitchen and watched us.

After a while Huey said, "This is hard work."

"That's too bad," my father said. "Your beating's not done!" And he added sugar and cream and lemon juice to Huey's pan and put the pan on the stove. And Huey went on beating.

"My arm hurts from whipping," I said.

"That's too bad," my father said. "Your whipping's not done."

So I whipped and whipped, and Huey beat and beat.

"Hold that beater in the air, Huey!" my father said.

Huey held it in the air.

"See!" my father said. "A good pudding stays on the beater. It's thick enough now. Your beating's done." Then he turned to me. "Let's see those egg whites, Julian!" he said.

They were puffed up and fluffy. "Congratulations, Julian!" he said. "Your whipping's done."

He mixed the egg whites into the pudding himself. Then he passed the pudding to my mother.

"A wonderful pudding," she said. "Would you like some, boys!"

"No thank you," we said.

She picked up a spoon. "Why, this tastes like a whole raft of lemons," she said. "This tastes like a night on the sea."

From *The Julian Stories*
by ANN CAMERON

Our City

What's that smell?
I've never smelled that before.
All hot and spicy and sweet
    smelling too,
Where does it come from?
Does it come from below
Or does it come from above?
You cannot tell in this flat.

Let's see now,
Above lives Mrs Ranji
New in from India.
Below lives that African fellow,
You know the one with the fat wife.

Sniff!   Sniff!   I've smelled that before.
Last Monday lunch time
In our school dining hall.
What was it we had now?
Minced beef and tomato-sauce?
No!   That was Tuesday.
That is a new foreign dish.
Curry it was called, spicy sweet
I like it, pleasant to taste.

Curry, hot on the tongue
Sweet with fruit and meat.
Now who eats curry?   Must be upstairs.
Mrs Ranji, she's Indian.
Indian people make curry.
I remember the taste.
Lovely taste.
If I go to borrow some tea
Perhaps Mrs Ranji
Would invite me to eat.
No, that's too much to ask,
Ah well, just beans and toast for me.

Tap, tap!   Who is that at the door now?
Oh Mrs Ranji, Hello!
What, for me?
A bowl of your lovely curry?
How can I refuse? Yes, yes!
What, come to your flat?
How can I refuse?

I enter ahead of my cook,
The air thick with heat and spice.
The family welcome me, I'm shy,
They sit me down,
The cloth a brilliant white
The curry a rich brown.
I dip my spoon,
All eyes on my action.

I lift, close my eyes and sip
From silver spoon.
I taste
I swallow smooth liquid,
Chew on the meat and rice
My taste buds rejuvenated
They come to life
The bitter-sweet spicy taste explodes.
I smile, they smile,
We eat silently
Each with their own thoughts,
Theirs on their own country
Mine on the baked beans
Still locked up in the tin.

MICHELLE PRENDERGAST (10)

Some People

Some people are black and some are white.
And this is to their delight.
From the country of origin,
To religion and customs,
And different foods and colours too.

It does not matter how they dress or how they
   speak
And what languages they have.
So really black and white are the same.
If they are in a fight try to stop it.
If they have a cut
It will mend.
And that way you get a new friend.

NICOLA JEFFREY (11)

The Mouse Girl

CAST:
Mouse (-girl)   Clouds   Forest-mouse
Hermit   Wind   Chorus
Sun   Mountain   Narrator

SCENE: India
TIME: Long ago

MOUSE: Help! Help! Won't someone
    save me? Help!

CHORUS: The mouse has been caught by a
    fierce kite. Someone come quickly.
    Quickly!

The cry for help was heard by a holy man, a
hermit.

HERMIT: What is it? Who cries? Ah,
    wicked kite, leave.

The hermit muttered a few magic words. The
kite dropped the mouse and flew away.

HERMIT: Are you hurt?

MOUSE: No. I thank you. I am only
    shaken. You saved my life. Let me
    stay with you in your protection.

HERMIT: I should like that. Come, I will
    show you my cave.

The hermit grew very fond of the mouse. One day he said:

HERMIT: She's too good to be a mouse. I shall turn her into a maiden.

He muttered more magic words and the mouse turned into a beautiful girl.

MOUSE-GIRL: I thank you for what you have done. But now that I am a girl I cannot stay with you. You are not my father. It would not be right.

HERMIT: I know this. You need a husband. A very powerful husband. I will find you one.

MOUSE-GIRL: But who is more powerful than you?

HERMIT: The sun. I shall speak to the sun. Sun, can you hear me?

SUN: I can hear everything. What do you want?

HERMIT: This maiden needs your protection. You have no wife. Will you marry her?

The sun, however, was basking in its own heat and was not the least interested in marrying the girl.

SUN: But I'm not so powerful as the clouds. They cover me up and block out my heat. Ask one of them.

CHORUS: And that was his excuse!

HERMIT: I shall speak to the clouds.
Clouds, can you hear me?

CLOUDS: We hear everything.

HERMIT: Then will one of you marry this
maiden and give her your protection?

CLOUDS: Ah, but we are not so powerful as
the wind. Have you asked the wind?
He pushes and pulls us around and breaks
us up all the time. Ask the wind.

CHORUS: And that was their excuse!

HERMIT: Then I shall speak to the wind,
and perhaps we shall be lucky. Wind,
can you hear me?

WIND: I hear everything. What do you
want?

HERMIT: You are more powerful than the
sun and the clouds. You must marry
this maiden and give her your protection.

The wind turned over lazily. He was much too
happy roaming the world to settle down with a
wife.

WIND: I am not so powerful as you think.
Why, nothing can make the mountain
move a hair's breadth – however hard I
puff. Ask the mountain.
CHORUS: And that was his excuse!

The hermit sighed, but turned to the mountain.

HERMIT: Mountain, they say you are the
          most powerful being in the world.   This
          maiden needs your protection.   Won't
          you marry her?

MOUNTAIN: I?   The most powerful?
          Haven't you noticed my feet are riddled
          with mouse holes?   They eat into me and
          I can do nothing about it.   If you want
          protection go to the mice.   They are the
          strongest of all.

CHORUS: And that was his excuse!

This set the hermit pondering.   The world was
full of excuses, it seemed.   But there was some
truth in what the mountain said, so he went to a
forest-mouse.

HERMIT: Forest-mouse, all the beings of the
          earth and sky tell me you are the most
          powerful.   This maiden needs your
          protection.   Will you marry her?

FOREST-MOUSE: But she's much, much
          bigger than me.   How will she be able to
          get into my mouse hole – for that is where
          she shall live.

The hermit sighed again, this time with great
weariness.   He could take no more excuses.

HERMIT: Good, kind girl, who means so
          much to me, it is better I think that you

return to being a mouse.

Sadly, the hermit muttered a few powerful words over her and turned her back into a mouse before she could protest.   The hermit persuaded her to marry the forest-mouse who now thought the world of her, and off she went.   The hermit went back to his cave and thought hard about the world and its excuses.

CHORUS: And the moral of that story is – well, work it out for yourself!

Adapted by RICHARD BROWN from a folk-tale in
Folk Tales of All Nations, edited by F. LEE

My Grandfather in Cyprus

I'd like to meet my Grandad
But he lives in a land far away,
Where it is hot and sunny.
I hear he is an old man now,
His face is wrinkled like a lemon in the sun.
When we meet
We will talk in Greek,
Someday.

MICHAEL XENOFONTOS (11)

My Island Dream

My holiday in St. Vincent
Meeting my grandad.

Chicken, rice and peas on Sundays,
A smashing dinner,
Playing with my cousin Arle
Messing about in the yard.

I'd love to go back to Parkhill
And work on the farm

My dream of a sunshine island.
BRIAN COLLINS (12)

Wriggly and the Big Orange Moon

Late one afternoon Wriggly squeezed herself through the gap in the back paling and made her way down to the beach with her skipping rope. The rope was made from a piece of fresh vine and Wriggly liked running and skipping with it along the damp sea shore.

So, doing just that, and taking little notice of anything else, like the disappearing sun or the lengthening shadows of the courida trees, Wriggly skipped and ran and skipped and ran. Suddenly, she spotted a round silver coin half-buried in the brown sandy beach.

With a flip of her heart Wriggly bent down and quickly dug it out with a bit of wet branch. It was a twenty-five cent piece and Wriggly could hardly believe her luck as she wiped it clean on the edge of her dress.

It was the first time she had ever found so much money.

Wriggly gripped the cold coin tightly in her fist, her fingers gently searching out all the little ridges that ran around it. Her mind flashed from sugarcakes to toffee to red iced fruities, and finally came to rest on something her mother was always telling her to keep, a puzzling-tin, to save up her money in.

Thoughts of a puzzling-tin, brimming with money, were full in Wriggly's head as she dropped her vine-rope on the beach and began to head back home. Her heart warmed whenever she felt the hard coin in her pocket. But it was getting late and Wriggly could not see a single other person in sight.

Wriggly quickened her footsteps. She was just passing another dark clump of courida trees when she looked up and saw a huge orange ball staring down at her from between the trees. Wriggly gasped at the sight and it was some moments before she realised it was the moon.

But it was so big and shone with such a strange glow that Wriggly just stood there staring at it. She had never seen the moon like that before. And as Wriggly gazed at it she also noticed a funny pinkish tint about the skies and a queer silence about the trees and the shore.

Now, Wriggly's imagination was such that it wasn't long before she began to put two and two together, her heart pounding all the while. Perhaps the moon was a sign. A sign that the world was going to end. Her Sunday School teacher had told her all about it. That one day the world would end and Jesus and his angels would burst through the skies, and a loud trumpet would be sounded.

Wriggly became cold at the thought of it, and the next moment she was running, faster than the speed of lightning, her heart doing a mad somersault within her chest, her feet almost tripping her up in their haste. Wriggly never stopped running until she came to the back steps of their home. There, she sat down panting and began to pray. "Please God, forgive me for all the bad things I've done and please save me and let me go up to heaven. Please save my mother and father and all my friends. Please, please, please."

Then Wriggly's hand closed around the twenty-five cent coin in her pocket, and the thought came to her that she should put this in the collection plate at church on Sunday, and maybe God wouldn't worry to end the world after all.

Just then, Wriggly heard her mother calling. Sick with fear she made her way up the steps.

"Whatever's the matter with you?" asked her mother, glancing at her face.

"Nothing, Mummy," said Wriggly, trying to squeeze some warmth back into her hands. She wanted to tell her mother all about it, but at the same time she wasn't quite certain. What if the world wasn't going to end? Her mother would laugh at her. Wriggly clutched the coin in her pocket and waited.

Suddenly she could help it no longer, and burst out, "Mummy, look at the moon at the window."

Wriggly's mother got up slowly and went towards the window. After what seemed like the longest while, Wriggly heard her voice exclaiming, "What a beautiful moon! I don't think I've ever seen it so nice and big before."

Wriggly felt the warm blood rushing to her hands and face again, her fears disappearing all in one rush. How foolish she was. Just imagine her forgetting about a full moon.

Wriggly became so cheerful after that she began to tell her mother about the coin and the puzzling-tin which she was going to keep. Gone were her thoughts of putting it in the collection plate on Sunday. Instead, Wriggly reached up on the shelf for an empty cocoa tin, made a slit in the lid with the cutter and dropped her coin inside.

The coin stayed at the bottom of the tin until Friday, when Wriggly couldn't resist taking it to school to show her friends. Sunday came and she still hadn't put the coin back into the tin.

She dressed herself for church in her pink cotton dress and new white socks, and as the coin was lying in the pocket of her school kimono, she took it out and dropped it into the pocket of her dress.   Though Wriggly went to morning church with her mother and father, she also went to Sunday School which was held in the afternoon.

Church was held at the Lowdam School and the small platform which her father sat on during the week became the pulpit every Sunday.   Sometimes Wriggly's father took the service and her mother played the old creaky organ beside the platform.

When they were ready for church Wriggly's mother handed her the usual five-cent coin to throw as collection.

There was a good turn out at church that morning, as the people of Lowdam believed in coming to church, especially the older ones. Wriggly, who liked sitting at the very front, called out to Daddy Abel and Cousin Rose and Uncle Joe and Aunt May, and all the other people, as she walked down the aisle to her seat.

Wriggly felt warm and contented inside. She liked the way the sunshine came through the small coloured glass window at the top. The colours were a deep blue and a light yellow and a bright orange, and they fell on the lily-white table cloth that Aunt May had spread on her father's table.

Wriggly settled herself in her seat and felt very proud of her father, preaching, and her mother, playing the organ, though she wished that her father didn't speak so long.   At times he went on and on about things she didn't quite understand.   Wriggly enjoyed the hymn singing however, and even though she never knew all the words of the hymns, she sang to the tune, putting in her own words.

That morning her father spoke about the sower who went forth to sow seeds.   In between drawing circles with her finger, Wriggly listened to him.   She tried to imagine how a sower could sow seeds into the ground because she knew her mother always sewed with a needle and thread.   When her father came to the bit where the seeds that were sown on good soil sprang up, Wriggly thought this was going too far.   How could seeds jump out of the earth?

Wriggly was still deep in thought about this when she suddenly realised that Uncle Joe was holding the gleaming collection plate under her nose.   Wriggly fumbled quickly in her pocket, then dropped a shiny coin into the polished plate.   Uncle Joe, who always took the collection, smiled at her and moved towards the platform in his brown Sunday suit.

But the next moment Wriggly was leaping up in alarm, because instead of putting the five-cent piece her mother had given her, she had put the shiny twenty-five cent coin she had found on the beach.

Uncle Joe had just reached the platform when he heard Wriggly's urgent voice beside him, "Uncle Joe! Please let me get my twenty-five cents from the collection plate."

Wriggly's voice sounded loud in the quiet church. Uncle Joe stared at her as if he wasn't quite certain what to do and everyone else also

stared at her.   Wriggly certainly knew what to do however, and her hand was reaching for the collection plate when she heard the low voice of her father.   "Go back to your seat," he said, taking hold of the plate.

Wriggly stared at him, then without another word went back to her seat and sat down hard. More hymns were sung, but Wriggly remained in her seat, her throat feeling tight with tears she refused to shed.

Then in a short while church was over and people were crowding around her father and mother.   Uncle Joe and Daddy Abel came hurrying to comfort her, but Wriggly rushed out of church.

She was thinking of her shiny twenty-five cent coin and the puzzling-tin, as she made her way home, and she was thinking how unfair it was.   But then, all of a sudden, Wriggly remembered that late afternoon on the beach and the big frightening moon and she began to feel relieved that she had thrown the coin. Perhaps God wouldn't end the world for a long time to come.

From *Trust You Wriggly*
by GRACE NICHOLLS

Linda's Lie

Linda's parents cannot afford to give her £1.00 to pay for a school trip to the ballet. Linda does not want to admit this so she tells a lie. "I'm going to a christening on that day," she tells her teacher. But that isn't true.

At home, the last thing Linda wanted was any talk of ballet, or dancing, or theatres. Even school seemed a dangerous subject to get on. She didn't want her father angry about the outing, or sorry. She didn't want her mother taking her side or her brother Michael asking questions. She had started something off – something bad – and all she wanted now was for next Monday to come and go with nothing said.

She'd have liked to hibernate till Tuesday. But she couldn't do that. She had to stew inside and act normal.

That evening she sat in front of the television in dread of *Blue Peter* doing a bit about the ballet. Or of Michael kicking his leg over the chair arm and asking whose room she'd go in when her class was out. She didn't want him looking for her in school that day.

What did you *do* out of school all day anyway? Someone could see you – even your father, when he was out looking for work!

Her heart turned over when he came in. It was horrible. She wasn't pleased to see him. She had to act it. Is this what being a liar's like? she thought. This nasty pain all the time, and not being able to look straight at your dad?

And he seemed all full of himself today – taller in the doorway. But he didn't say why, not to her, nor to Michael. He looked at the TV set, hummed a little something deep in his throat and went out to the kitchen.

It was bed-time before Linda found out what it was. And then it wasn't her father who told her. He wasn't a showy man.

"Look!" said her mother as she tucked Linda in on the lumpy mattress. She held out a shiny pound piece. "This is for your outing. Your daddy got it extra today. Did a little job for a man he met. We won't miss it, being extra." She was smiling such a happy smile.

Linda looked up at the coin. It should have looked good and made her smile, but it didn't. It looked like money from another country. Even the Queen looked cross as if she was saying, "We've found you out, Linda Ann Steel. Look where lying leads you. . . ."

Linda's eyes filled with tears. She put her head under the blankets to hide them – and she suddenly felt like their silent canary must feel – covered, and trapped: only she was in a cage of lies.

"Ah – don't cry, Petal." Her mother patted the mound of her head. "It's a happy ending to the story, eh?"

The next day

The cold coin in Linda's sock seemed to stick out like some nasty bite. You could see it if you knew where to look for it, even with white socks on. And you'd see where it had been when she took them off for dance, grazing her all grey where it scratched her ankle.

But she didn't know what else to do with it. She couldn't just give it in and say she was going to the ballet after all. Not really. They didn't cancel christenings just like that, and she'd made it sound much too important to just have changed her mind.

There was nowhere to hide it at home where someone wouldn't come across it – and nobody's place was secret enough in school. The only other thing would be to throw it away. But she shivered at the thought. A picture in her head of her father working for it made the money much too precious for that.

It weighed her down as if it had been in pennies. Why had she had to tell Miss Smith a lie? It had seemed easy at first, but now it was getting harder and harder every minute.

With her bag held against her leg she went into the classroom. Today she really didn't want to be at school. But if she thought things were bad, there was worse to come. Life could play some terrible tricks.

"Listen, children, I've got something important to ask you. Andrew Field has lost his ballet money. He thinks he left it in his bag in the cloakroom – silly boy – but he's just been back to look, and it isn't there."

Everyone looked at Andrew Field, mouths in little O's. He put on a tragic face and stared at his *Happy Reader*. Then they looked for Jason Paris: but he was late again. He'd kick his way into the classroom in a minute – in a mood, but innocent!

"Mind you, Andrew could have dropped it somewhere else. So if anyone comes across it

I'll be very grateful."

Linda remembered past fusses about missing things. A feeling of nobody being trusted would hang in the classroom till the money was found, or it was forgotten.

"Anyway, it's our hall time now, so let's get changed for it quickly and quietly."

Now Linda had to take her socks off. And just as she knew it would, the pound piece in the right one seemed to burn like something jumped out from a bonfire. If anyone saw that now it would be much too late to say she'd brought her money to go after all. There'd be all sorts of questions asked, and Donna Paget would think it was Christmas. They'd have to talk to her parents to clear it up, and then all the christening lie would come out.

"Hurry up, Linda. Come on, it's not like you to be slow for dance."

But getting off a sock with money in it was every bit as difficult as Linda thought it would be. The hard-edged lump kept riding up with her leg and seemed to want to jump itself out and onto the floor. And trapping it between her thumb and her sock only left that guilty secret showing in her hand.

There was only one last chance. She pretended the sock was too tight and did the other one instead. If she hid the money leg, she told herself, she could do it while the others went out of the room.

She pulled her dress over her head, folded it with the one sock hidden, and sat up straight with her arms on the desk.   Ready.   The whole room was ready.

"Good."   Miss Smith stood up.

"Please, Miss, Linda Steel's left one sock on!"   Donna Paget sounded as if she'd discovered a new planet.   And everyone laughed as if it was the best joke ever invented. Even Andrew Field forgot he was supposed to be worried sick about his money.

Linda closed her eyes.   Tight, dry, guilty eyes.

"Come on," said Miss Smith.   "Silly girl. Clocks won't stop for you."   She hurried in a zig-zag between the tables.   "Cock your leg up."

There was nothing else Linda could do.   She was done for.   Inside she had that empty, helpless feeling of just going off under gas at the dentist's.   She felt Miss Smith lift her foot, and

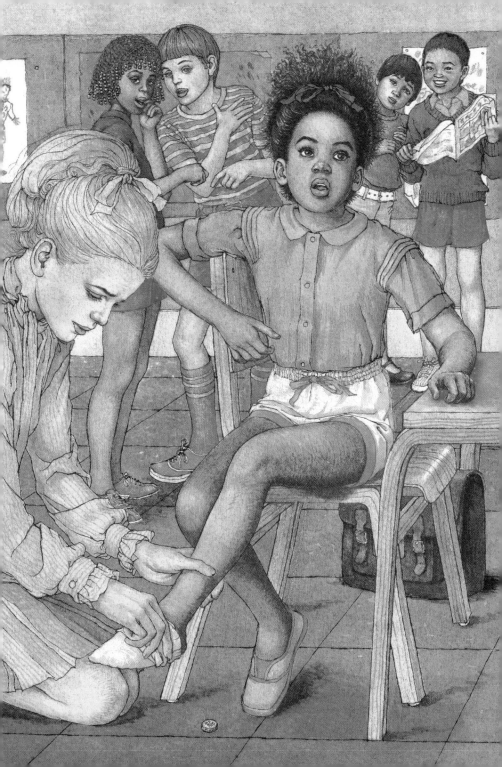

she thought she heard her own voice saying something beginning with "I . . ." She could hear the class laughing at the sight of Miss Smith helping her. But no noise was loud enough to cover the sound of the pound as its hard, ringing edge hit the floor.

"Whee, Miss. . ."

"Linda Steel!"

"Hey, look, Andrew. . ."

Public shock. Private glee. Even good friends drew in their breath.

"I think you'd better take this money and have a little talk with Mrs. Cheff, Linda," said Miss Smith. "Don't you?"

Linda's father rings the school to check that she is able to go on the trip. The headmistress finds Andrew's missing coin in the cloakroom – so she knows Linda did not steal the coin. Linda could have kept quiet about her lie but she told everything to the kind headmistress. She felt much better after that.

From *Linda's Lie*
by BERNARD ASHLEY

The Twelve Days of Christmas

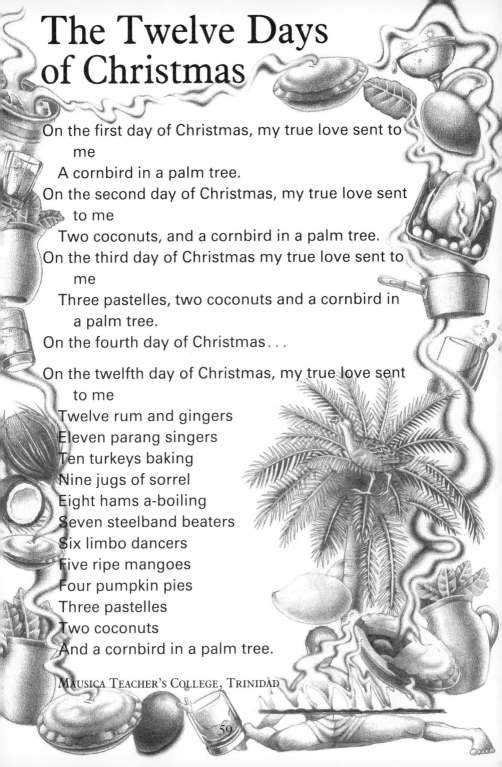

On the first day of Christmas, my true love sent to me
  A cornbird in a palm tree.
On the second day of Christmas, my true love sent to me
  Two coconuts, and a cornbird in a palm tree.
On the third day of Christmas my true love sent to me
  Three pastelles, two coconuts and a cornbird in a palm tree.
On the fourth day of Christmas...

On the twelfth day of Christmas, my true love sent to me
  Twelve rum and gingers
  Eleven parang singers
  Ten turkeys baking
  Nine jugs of sorrel
  Eight hams a-boiling
  Seven steelband beaters
  Six limbo dancers
  Five ripe mangoes
  Four pumpkin pies
  Three pastelles
  Two coconuts
  And a cornbird in a palm tree.

MAUSICA TEACHER'S COLLEGE, TRINIDAD

59

The Woman, the Boy and the Lion

Once, long ago in Ethiopia, there lived a woman named Fanaye who was a widow. After a while she married a good sort of man whose wife had died, leaving him with one little boy.

So now the little boy had a stepmother. I don't know why it was – perhaps he had heard tales about bad stepmothers – but anyhow this little boy would hardly speak to Fanaye, just turned his head away if he saw that she was looking at him and never said good night or good morning or let her kiss him.

Now this Fanaye was a nice woman. She hadn't got any children of her own and she had thought how nice it would be to have this little boy to look after.

But no! Do what she would, however hard she tried she couldn't get the little boy to be friends with her, not even if she cooked specially nice food for him or tried to cuddle him and tell him stories.

Poor Fanaye asked all her friends what she ought to do, but none of them could suggest anything new, just all the things she had tried already.

Her husband often had to go away on long

journeys and she was afraid that he would begin
to think that she had been unkind to his little son.

At last she went to the Wise Man.

"What am I to do!" she said. "My little
stepson doesn't love me!" And she told the
Wise Man about all the things she had tried,
and how the little boy didn't eat his food, and
how, if she tried to pick him up and kiss him,
the child only struggled away and burst into
tears.

"Help me, if you can, O Wise Man. My
husband is sure to believe I am being unkind to
his little son."

"I think I can help you," said the Wise Man after thinking. "But I shall most likely need to make a very strong spell. Now for the spell you will have to bring me some hairs from the tail of a black-maned lion. Mind! You must get the hairs yourself, otherwise the spell won't work. Bring them as soon as you can."

Poor Fanaye didn't know what to do. None of the tame lions were the black-maned kind! She herself wasn't very big or very brave and she was dreadfully afraid of the wild lions and always ran as fast as she could past a certain lion's cave on the side of the mountain, a cave that she had to pass when she went down the mountain to get water from the spring. Now and then she could hear this lion roaring inside the cave and every night they were careful to shut up their cow and calf safely in the shed for fear this lion should kill them. The dangerous time was when the lion came out of his cave and prowled about at dusk.

So when the Wise Man said that, the poor woman thought how could she ever come near a lion, still less get hairs from his tail? So she went home very down-hearted. But that evening it was just the same with the little boy. He wouldn't speak to her, he turned his head away if she looked at him, wouldn't eat the supper she had cooked for him and crept away to bed without a word.

Well, that was dreadful.   So at last she said to herself, "I will try to do it!"

But how?   All that night she thought and thought and at last she decided on a plan. Next evening she took some meat with her when she went (rather late) to get water and, on her way home again, she left the meat at the mouth of the lion's cave, but she was too frightened to wait and see what would happen.

Next evening she did the same thing but this time she didn't run away but hid behind a tree to watch.   Sure enough, after a while, the lion came out, saw the meat, sniffed at it and then lay down comfortably to eat it holding the meat between his paws.   She saw that he was a big black-maned lion.   He moved his tail about as he ate and the hairs at the end of this tail of his were black too.

"Oh dear," she thought, "the Wise Man would have known if I'd tried cheating and gone to the town – to Debre Marcos – and got one of the keepers to give me hairs off the tail of one of the Emperor's tame lions."

She thought this black-maned wild lion was a beautiful beast but she was very much afraid of him.

Next day – that was the third day – she brought meat again and this time, the third

time, she stood waiting, still a good way off, but where the lion could see her.

On the fourth evening she sat down much nearer, and on the fifth evening she held out the meat to him in her hand – but she had to drop it at the last minute.

So it went on, till after a while there came a day when the lion was taking meat from her quite peaceably.

At last (very carefully, so as not to pull), she was able to snip, each day, a few of the beautiful hairs from the end of his tail while he contentedly crunched meat and bone. When she had got a nice little bunch, Fanaye – very well pleased –

went off to the Wise Man again.

"Here is the hair from the lion's tail that you asked for," she said to him, holding it out. "What must I do now?"

"Well done, Fanaye," said the Wise Man. "It must have been quite difficult!   How did you manage it?"

So then Fanaye told the Wise Man all about it – how she had brought meat and put it outside the lion's cave but how at first she had been too frightened even to see if he would eat it and how she had run away.   Then how, day by day, she had gone on bringing meat and had come a little nearer and how, soon, he would take the meat quite peaceably from her hand and how, in the end, he had allowed her to cut, each day, a tail hair or two and how careful she had had to be not to pull.

"That was very well done!" said the Wise Man.   "You were very careful, you didn't startle him and so in the end he trusted you. The spell you asked for?   You know it now. Make friends slowly; don't startle him.   Surely it will be easier with a human child than with a wild, black-maned lion?"

And so it was.   Fanaye was very patient, but at last the little boy got quite friendly, ate his food nicely and used to sit on her lap while she told him stories.

And the story he liked best was one about a wild black-maned lion.

From *The Story Spirits*
By A WILLIAMS-ELLIS

My Friends

I have four good friends around my flats,
We all live on the same estate.
Their names are George, Ibrahim, Nazia and Paul,
We are good friends.
George is a Chinese boy who likes to muck about,
But at the same time he's very quiet –
He's like a lion cub, quiet but playful.
Ibrahim is a Turkish boy who comes from Cyprus.
He's like a wildcat sometimes.
Nazia is a Mauritian, he comes from Mauritius.
He puts on an act like a tiger.
Paul is an English boy who looks cool,
He's like a panther, ready to pounce.
I am like a cat, quiet and happy.
Ibrahim and me are friends
Although he is Turkish and I am Greek,
We come from countries all around the world,
We make new links together like links on a chain,
We share together our happiness and pain.

MICHAEL XENOFONTOS
DEAN COVENTRY (13)

The Cherry Tree

*At the start of the story Rakesh is six.   He lives by
the Himalayan Mountains in Northern India with
his grandfather.   His mother and father live fifty
miles away but Rakesh stays with his grandfather
in order to attend the nearby school – for there is
no school near his parents' home.   There are not
many fruit trees near Grandfather's house.
Rakesh plants a cherry stone in the garden.*

   The story begins the following spring.

One morning in the garden, he bent to pick up what he thought was a small twig and found to his surprise that it was well rooted. He stared at it for a moment, then ran to fetch Grandfather, calling "*Dada*, come and look, the cherry tree has come up!"

"What cherry tree?" asked Grandfather, who had forgotten about it.

"The seed we planted last year – look, it's come up!"

Rakesh went on his knees, while Grandfather bent double and peered down at the tiny tree. It was about ten centimetres high.

"Yes, it's a cherry tree all right," said Grandfather. "You must water it now and then."

Rakesh watered it and circled it with pebbles.

"What are the pebbles for?" asked Grandfather.

"For privacy," said Rakesh.

He looked at the tree every morning, but it did not seem to be growing very fast. So he stopped looking at it – except quickly, out of the corner of his eye. And after a week or two, when he allowed himself to look at it properly, he found that it *had* grown – at least three centimetres!

That year the monsoon rains came early, and Rakesh plodded to and from school in his raincoat and gumboots. Ferns grew from the rocks, strange-looking lilies came up in the long grass, and even when it wasn't raining, the trees dripped and mist came curling up the valley. The cherry tree grew quickly.

When the tree was about sixty centimetres high, a goat entered the garden and ate all the young leaves. Rakesh spotted the goat as he was coming down the path. He chased it out of the garden and all the way down the hill until it leapt across a small ravine; but when he returned to the garden, out of breath and still very angry, he found that only the cherry tree's main stem and two thin branches remained.

"Never mind," said Grandfather, seeing that Rakesh was upset. "It will grow again, cherry trees are tough."

Towards the end of the rainy season new leaves appeared on the tree. And then one day a woman cutting grass came scrambling down the hillside, her scythe swishing through everything that came in the way. One sweep, and the cherry tree was cut in two.

Grandfather saw what had happened. He went up to the woman and scolded her.

"What do you mean by cutting our tree?" he demanded.

"I didn't see it," said the woman. "I was cutting the grass."

"You weren't looking," said Grandfather. "And anyway, who asked you to cut our grass?"

"It was long. It needed cutting. I'm taking it home for my cows!"

"You won't cut any of our grass without my permission," fumed Grandfather. "And besides, I like long grass. I like looking at it. I like walking on it. I like sitting on it."

The woman went away muttering something about the old man being crazy. Grandfather bent over the cherry tree and examined it closely; it looked as though the damage could not be repaired.

"Maybe it will die now," said Rakesh, looking downcast.

"Maybe," said Grandfather.

*   *   *   *   *

The cherry tree had no intention of dying. By the time summer came round again, it had sent out several new shoots with tender green leaves. Rakesh had grown taller, too. He was eight now, a sturdy boy with curly hair and deep black eyes. "Blackberry eyes," Grandfather called them. They were like the wild blackberries growing on the hillside.

The berries ripened in July. Rakesh collected a bagful of them, and Grandfather made blackberry jam – three jars, which lasted through the summer.

Another monsoon came and went, and during it Rakesh went home to his village, to help his father and mother with the ploughing and sowing and planting. He was thinner but stronger when he came back to Grandfather's house at the end of the rains, to find that the cherry tree had grown another thirty centimetres. It was now up to his chest.

Even when there was plenty of rain, Rakesh would sometimes water the tree. He wanted it to know that he was *there*.

One day he found a bright green praying-mantis perched on a branch, peering at him with bulging eyes. It was the cherry tree's first visitor. It would not harm the tree. On the contrary, it was soon busy snapping up all the

leaf-cutting insects that came its way.

Next day there was another visitor – a hairy caterpillar who started making a meal of several leaves. Rakesh removed it quickly and dropped it over the wall. He had learnt at school about ugly caterpillars turning into beautiful butterflies, so he didn't want to kill it; nor did he want it eating up all the leaves.

He watched the caterpillar crawl away, and said, "Come back when you're a butterfly."

Winter came early that year. The cherry tree bent low with the weight of snow. Field-mice sought shelter in the roof of the cottage.

In February it was Rakesh's birthday. He was nine – and the tree was four, but almost as tall as Rakesh. They had a tea-party in the garden – Grandfather was good at tea-parties – and Rakesh's friends came and ate up everything there was to eat, and then they sang and danced round the cherry tree and played hide-and-seek on the hillside until it grew dark.

One morning, when the sun came out, Grandfather came into the garden to 'let some warmth into my bones,' as he put it. He stopped in front of the cherry tree, stared at it for a few seconds, and then called out, "Rakesh! Come and look! Quickly, before it falls!"

Rakesh dashed outside, wondering if the

house was falling down.   He found Grandfather
staring at the tree as if it had performed a
miracle.   There was a pale pink blossom at the
end of a branch.

*   *   *   *   *

The seasons passed, turning the forest from
light green to dark green to red to brown to
gold, and in the following year there were more
blossoms.   And then the tree was taller than
Rakesh, even though it was less than half his age.
And then it was taller than Grandfather who
was older than some of the oak and maple trees.

Rakesh had grown too.   He could run and
jump and climb trees better than most boys,
and he read a lot of books, although he still
liked listening to Grandfather's tales.

In the cherry tree, bees came to feed on the
nectar, and tiny birds pecked at the blossoms
and broke them off.   But the tree kept flowering
right through the spring, and there were always
more blossoms than birds.

That summer there were small cherries on the
tree.   Rakesh tasted one and spat it out.

"It's too sour," he said.

"They'll be better next year," said
Grandfather.

But the birds liked them.   Yellow-bottomed
bulbuls and scarlet minivets flitted in and out of
the foliage, feasting on the sour cherries.

On a warm sunny afternoon, when even the bees seemed drowsy, Rakesh looked out of the bedroom window and saw Grandfather reclining on a cane chair under the cherry tree. It was the first time Grandfather had taken his easy chair into the garden.

"There's just the right amount of shade here," he said. "And I like looking up at the leaves."

"They're bright shiny leaves," said Rakesh. "And they spin like tops when there's a breeze."

After Grandfather had gone indoors, Rakesh came into the garden and began weeding the flower-beds. When he was tired he lay down on the grass beneath the cherry tree. He gazed up through the leaves at the great blue sky; and turning on his side, he could see the mountains striding away into the clouds. He was still lying beneath the tree when the evening shadows crept across the garden. Grandfather came back and sat down beside Rakesh, and they waited in silence until the stars came out and the night-jar began to call. In the forest below, the crickets and cicadas began shrilling and squeaking like an orchestra tuning up; then they all started playing together, and the trees were filled with the sound of insects.

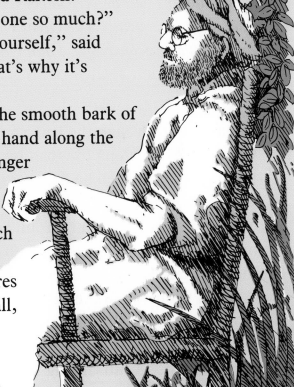

"So many trees in the forest," mused Rakesh. "Why do I like this one so much?"

"You planted it yourself," said Grandfather. "That's why it's special."

Rakesh touched the smooth bark of the tree. He ran his hand along the trunk and put his finger to the tip of a leaf. He reached up and was just able to touch the highest branch.

"Nearly two metres tall," he said. "Tall, strong cherry, all grown by me!"

From *The Cherry Tree*
by Ruskin Bond

Chin Chiang and the Dragon Dance

Chin Chiang, a Chinese boy, has long wanted to dance with his grandfather Wu in the giant dragon costume and mask. The dance is on the first day of the Chinese New Year and Chin Chiang's job is to be the tail of the dragon while his grandfather is the head. But the boy is afraid that he will dance badly. He has been told that the Great Dragon in the mountains will be very angry with anyone who does not dance well. The Great Dragon can send high winds and flooding. Chin Chiang becomes afraid. He runs away from his grandfather's house . . .

Looking out through the lantern mask, Chin Chiang hurried along the road by the sea to the public library, which he had visited many times when he wanted to be alone. He opened the door and ran up the stairs, round and round, higher and higher, up, up, up, to the door at ` the top that led out to the roof.

From his perch in the sky he could see the mountains rising above the sea and below him the animal lanterns, which would glow like tiny stars tonight. Chin Chiang felt happier than he had for many days.

"I never expected to meet a rabbit on top of this roof," called a strange voice.

Chin Chiang turned around quickly. A woman carrying a mop and pail was coming towards him.

"I'm not a rabbit," he said shyly. "I am Chin Chiang," and he pulled off the lantern.

"Oh, that is much better," she said. "Greetings, Chin Chiang. My name is Pu Yee. May I enjoy the view with you?" She didn't wait for a reply. "In a little while I'll be watching the New Year's parade from here. I used to dance the dragon's dance when I was young, but not any more. My feet are too old, and they are covered with corns."

"My grandfather dances the dragon's dance," said Chin Chiang, "and his corns are as old as yours."

Pu Yee laughed. "His old shoes may move his old bones, but my feet will never dance again."

A wonderful idea suddenly came to Chin Chiang. What if he had found someone to take his place in the dance? He would show Pu Yee his part in the dance right now. No one would see them if they tripped or fell.

"You can help me practise what my grandfather taught me," he said.

"Oh, my creaky bones, what a funny sight

this will be," said Pu Yee.

"You *can* dance," he told her. Cautiously
Chin Chiang gave a little jump. Pu Yee
jumped too. He shook slowly at first and she
shook too. Next they leaped into the air,
landed together and spun on their heels.

Before long Pu Yee had forgotten her creaky
bones.   Then Chin Chiang stumbled and fell.
   "Let's try again," said Pu Yee, picking him up.
   While they danced, darkness crept down
slowly from the mountains to the
city below. Then, from far off,
Chin Chiang heard the lilting
tune of pigeons with whistles
tied to their tail feathers.

They had been set free from their cages in the marketplace and were flying high above the buildings. Chin Chiang knew this meant that the New Year Festival had begun.

"We must go, Pu Yee. We're late," said Chin Chiang. "The pigeons are flying free."

"I'm not late," she replied. "I'm staying here."

But Chin Chiang pulled her by the hand, and they hurried down the stairs together – round and round, down, down, down, to the market street. The sound of firecrackers exploded in their ears while the eager crowd buzzed and hummed. Chin Chiang pushed his way forward, but Pu Yee pulled back. In the noise and confusion Chin Chiang let go of her hand, and suddenly he came face to face with the dragon whose head was wreathed in smoke.

"Where have you been, Chin Chiang? I have been sick with worry," called Grandfather Wu in a muffled voice. Chin Chiang did not reply. "Come now, take up the tail before the smoke disappears and everyone can see us."

Chin Chiang stood still, his feet frozen to the ground. The clamour of the street grew louder, stinging his ears. "I can't dance, Grandfather," he said.

Grandfather Wu turned away. "You can dance, Chin Chiang. Follow me."

"Look, look. Here comes the dragon!"

called Mr Sing. The crowd sent up a cheer that bounced off windows and doors and jumped into the sky.

Chin Chiang was trapped. Slowly he stooped and picked up the tail. Grandfather Wu shook the dragon's head fiercely until Chin Chiang started to kick his heels to the beat of the thundering drum.

Then, suddenly, Chin Chiang stumbled, but instead of falling he did a quick step and recovered his balance. Excitedly, he leaped into the air, and again, and higher again. And as the dance went on, Chin Chiang's feet moved more surely, his steps grew firmer and his leaps more daring. Mrs Lau and Mr Koo cheered from their market shops while people poured out of their houses onto balconies and sidewalks, filling the streets. High in the sky flags of fire and falling moons burst into light. They sizzled and sparkled, rocketed straight up and whistled to the ground.

Just then, Chin Chiang caught sight of a familiar face in the crowd. It was Pu Yee. Chin Chiang leaped to the sidewalk, and pulled her into the street.

"I can't, Chin Chiang," she said, pulling away. "My bones. My corns. My knees."

"Pu Yee, yes, you can," Chin Chiang assured her. "Look at me!" Hesitantly she took hold of the tail and together they kicked up their heels just as they had on the rooftop, while the throngs of people cheered them on.   Up one street and down another they danced, to the beat of the thundering drum.

All too soon the dragon lifted its head and shook its tail for the last time.   The dance was over.   Pu Yee hugged Chin Chiang close.

Grandfather Wu smiled inside the dragon's head.   "Bring your new friend to our home for dinner, Chin Chiang," he said.   Pu Yee and Chin Chiang hopped quickly over the doorstep and into the bakeshop.

The family exchanged gifts of fine teas in wooden boxes, new clothes and small red envelopes of Lucky Money.   Then they sat together to share plates of meat dumplings and carp, bowls of steaming soup and trays of delicious pastries and cakes and fresh fruit.

"To Chin Chiang, the very best dragon's tail I have ever seen," said Grandfather Wu, raising his glass in a toast.

Chin Chiang's face glowed with pride.   "To a prosperous Year of the Dragon," he said, raising his glass to his mama, papa, grandfather and his new friend Pu Yee.

From *Chin Chiang and the Dragon Dance*
by IAN WALLACE

Lo-Sun, the Blind Boy

Many hundreds of years ago there lived in
China a boy called Lo-Sun.   He was blind.
His father hated the thought that one of his sons
should be blind and always dependent on the
family, and one day he threw the boy into the
street.   "Don't try to return," he warned.
"Our door is closed to you.   You must fend
for yourself, learn to be a beggar."   And with
those hard words he closed the door.

Lo-Sun, full of hate for his father, set off
down the dusty road to the city.   He carried a
blind man's stick and a begging bowl.   How
miserable he was going to be, he was thinking,
when suddenly he heard excited barking behind
him, and there running towards him was his
dog, Fan.   "Fan," he cried, delighted, "are you

coming with me?" The dog's tail waved back and forth in a frenzy.

Fan was very useful to Lo-Sun. The boy only had to snap his fingers three times and Fan would bow to the ground, showing great respect to any passer-by. This earned both of them enough food to live on.

They wandered the city and became well-known. When the weather grew warmer they set out for the country and slept in the cooler shadows of the trees.

One night Lo-Sun had a strange dream. A low voice said, "Lo-Sun, can you see me?"

The boy replied, "I am blind."

"It grieves me to hear that," the voice said softly. "But perhaps I can help you."

"Can you bring back my sight?" the boy asked, his heart leaping.

"I cannot do that, but I can show you how it might be possible for you to see again. Listen carefully. Each time you do something which is good a little amount of light will enter your eyes. The more good you do the more you will see. But, as you may guess, if you do anything which is not good you shall lose twice the light you have gained and your eyes will darken and darken again."

The voice faded. Lo-Sun awoke. He looked about him. Was there more light?

The sun warmed his face and Fan seemed unusually happy. He told the dog about his dream, knowing that Fan would understand nothing but the hope in his voice. "I shall do it," he exclaimed fiercely, "I shall do it. I shall show my cruel father that I am as good as any of my brothers."

They made their way back towards the city. A beggar, sitting at the city gate, thrust forward a bowl and begged, "Give me something that I may not starve, for I have lost the sight of my eyes."

Lo-Sun touched the beggar's hair. "I am blind too," he said softly. "I cannot help you." And he thought: will I be like this in years to come?

"Poor child," the beggar sighed. "But at least you have the use of your legs."

Lo-Sun was so moved by the thought of the beggar's useless legs, without further ado he fumbled in his clothes and brought out his only coin. It fell with a hollow ring in the beggar's bowl.

All at once there seemed a double spark of light in Lo-Sun's eyes. The blackness faded to a misty grey. "The dream," he cried. "It is coming true!" He was unable to move for joy.

That night he slept in a rackety old building known as the Beggars' Temple. There an old woman complained of hunger gnawing her belly like rat's teeth, and Lo-Sun gave her his last piece of bread. He sat still, feeling the grey mist in his eyes begin to glow with a pale light. The hunger that kept him awake that night was a small price to pay for this.

In the morning both boy and dog were very hungry. They set out early to beg for food but few people were about. Fan ran on ahead and, as luck would have it, he came across a fat old hen that did not seem to belong to anyone. Lo-Sun took the hen from Fan's mouth and patted the dog with words of praise. It did not take him long to sell the hen at the market for a fair price. But as the buyer counted the coins into Lo-Sun's hand, the boy's heart sunk. His eyes were darkening. By the time the last coin was in his palm he had lost all the light he had gained since his dream.

But he knew why. All day he enquired if anyone had lost a hen. Hunger made him feel faint and gnawed at his stomach, but he did not weaken, did not buy food with the money he had received for the hen. He curled up in exhausted sleep that night, unhappy but still hopeful. When morning came his eyes were soft glows again: wonderful!

Weeks passed. Lo-Sun took every chance to do good, and eventually his sight was good

enough to tell if someone approached or
something was in his path.   The shape was still
blurred, without detail, but to a blind boy this
was still like a miracle.

He had saved a little money, for he thought, very sensibly, that he would buy a pair of spectacles to correct his blurred vision. Then he would be able to see almost as well as his brothers.

As he made his way about the city he came across the crippled beggar who had been the first to receive his charity. "I am starving," cried the beggar, and his bones showed it. "Please help me."

"But I have only a few coins and I need those for my spectacles," Lo-Sun answered without thinking. Darkness fell over his eyes like a hood; it was like a soft blow upon the head. Lo-Sun staggered back, crying out his bitter regret. "I have lost half the light I gained," he cried, for it seemed as bad as that. Fan tried to lick his hands, to rub against him, but Lo-Sun's anger against himself grew darker than his eyes.

Blind with despair now, he set off with angry, stumbling strides to the river. Its roar drew him. The river was swollen and flowed fiercely for it was the rainy season. Lo-Sun sat on the bank and brooded. Should he throw himself into the water and end all his misery now? For this darkness would always haunt him however good he was, and he would live out a miserable life like the lame beggar. Perhaps there was

only one thing that prevented him from
throwing himself at the torrent: Fan. For who
would look after his faithful dog?

A sudden cry broke into his thoughts.
Someone shouted, "Look, a boat's capsized out
there. A man is drowning. He can't swim."
A crowd quickly gathered. Lo-Sun could see
and hear well enough to know that not one of
them had jumped in to save the man. Why did
they just stare? Were they all cowards? He
knew that given sight he would not have
hesitated to try and save the drowning

man.   "I would do it," he cried to himself.   But how?   Fan barked.   Fan would do it.   "My dog will save him," he shouted. Someone tried to dissuade him but Lo-Sun cried, "Fan, Fan, fetch him.   Save him," and he pushed the eager dog into the river.

The watchers on the bank described to Lo-Sun what was happening.   "She is swimming so powerfully . . . no sign of tiredness . . . she is nearing him . . . he keeps rising up from the water . . . he can see her . . . the dog's got hold of his robe . . . they are turning . . . what a struggle! that man must be a dead weight . . . they're coming . . . but so slowly . . . slowly. . . they're slowing down. . ."

Lo-Sun crouched on the bank and shouted encouragement to Fan with all the air in his lungs.   He sensed his beloved dog's acute danger, sensed the life and death struggle. "Come on, Fan," he urged over and over again.

"They're nearer ... almost ... almost..."

A man with a boat-hook threw out his line and it was hitched onto the man in the water who was white and spluttering.   Several hands hauled him in.

"Where's Fan?" Lo-Sun called frantically. For the dark blur that was Fan in Lo-Sun's eyes had suddenly disappeared into the torrent.

"She's gone under," a voice said apologetically.   "The current snatched her

away before we could get hold of her. Poor thing, she used up all her strength."

Lo-Sun was stunned. He felt his body turn to ice. He sunk to his knees and huddled in the mud moaning his disbelief and grief. A great wave of misery washed over him. A few people touched him in pity but did not stay, for after all he's only a beggar boy, they thought. Lo-Sun did not stir. Over and over he muttered the dog's name until it became a chant like a dull heart beat.

Sleep eventually overtook him.

When he woke he thought first of his dog – no lick on the face to rouse him, no brushing of a tail on his legs. But as he opened his eyes he was astonished, for light flooded in, sparkled like the sun on the river's surface, pure light that filled him with the shape and colour of willows and water and grass and clouds in the blue sky. He stared in wonder – he could see! And the world, though still not clear in detail, was so dazzling in its colour he could hardly take it in. Like a dream more vivid than a dozen dreams rolled into one.

As Lo-Sun sat marvelling, a man approached him uncertainly. After studying the boy for a minute, and looking even more puzzled, the stranger approached the boy who was staring at the glowing leaves of a bamboo. "My boy," he said, "are you the one who sent his dog to save me yesterday?"

A cold prickle ran down the back of Lo-Sun's head. He knew that voice. He turned his face fully towards the man who gave a startled cry.

"Is it Lo-Sun?" the man stuttered.

"It is I – father," Lo-Sun said, for that indeed, so it now appeared, was the man he had saved from drowning. Now for the first time he could look his father fully in the face.

"Lo-Sun, my boy," his father said, falling to his knees and clasping his son. "I was cruel and thoughtless to turn you out of our home. Was there ever a more vile father? After what I have done, can you forgive me?"

Lo-Sun felt a spurt of anger rise in his throat. This was the man who had thrown him in the gutter. This was the man who had caused the death of his dog. How he hated him. How he wished to curse him, to inflict on him all the hurt he had felt in his years of wandering. . . .

But just in time Lo-Sun bit back the bitter words. A soft, dreamlike voice whispered a warning. Lo-Sun swallowed his words and his anger. He smiled and touched his father's face. "Father, I forgive you," he said in a new voice. At those words the last edge of darkness, the last grey mist, fell from his eyesight and his

vision was crystal clear.   "Father, I am no
longer blind," he said.   "And though for you I
have lost my best companion, my faithful Fan, I
have discovered how beautiful the world is."

And the boy led his father home.

Adapted by Richard Brown from a story in
  Folk Tales of All Nations
ed. by F. LEE